The HERMIT CRAB

CARTER GOODRICH

SIMON & SCHUSTER BOOKS FOR YOUNG READERS

NEW YORK   LONDON   TORONTO   SYDNEY

SIMON & SCHUSTER BOOKS FOR YOUNG READERS ~ An imprint of Simon & Schuster Children's Publishing Division ~ 1230 Avenue of the Americas, New York, New York 10020 ~ Copyright © 2009 by Carter Goodrich ~ All rights reserved, including the right of reproduction in whole or in part in any form. ~ SIMON & SCHUSTER BOOKS FOR YOUNG READERS is a trademark of Simon & Schuster, Inc. ~ Book design by Dan Potash ~ The text for this book is set in Stonehouse. ~ The illustrations for this book are rendered in colored pencils and watercolor. ~ Manufactured in China ~ 0519 SCP

4   6   8   10   9   7   5   3

Library of Congress Cataloging-in-Publication Data ~ Goodrich, Carter. ~ The hermit crab / Carter Goodrich.—1st ed. ~ p. cm. ~ Summary: Absorbed in his search for food, a shy hermit crab, disguised in a fancy new shell, inadvertently rescues a flounder caught beneath a trap and wins the admiration of the other marine animals. ~ ISBN: 978-1-4169-3892-7 (hardcover) ~ [1. Hermit crabs—Fiction. 2. Crabs—Fiction. 3. Marine animals—Fiction. 4. Humorous stories.] 1. Title. ~ PZ7.G61447Her 2009 ~ [E]—dc22 ~ 2007045240

For Allie, Coby, and Jack, with love

The hermit crab in this story didn't set out to be a hero. And he wasn't particularly brave. He was, actually, very shy. Whenever all his neighbors would get together, the hermit crab was happy to linger just out of sight. If anyone did happen to notice him, he would become terribly nervous and start to fidget. And then, if they should happen to say something like "Hi" or "How's it going?" he would disappear deep into his shell without saying a word.

Early one morning, just when the hermit crab's neighbors were sitting down to have breakfast, a large wooden contraption fell out of the sky and headed right for them. It bounced and clattered and finally came to rest smack-dab in the middle of their town square.

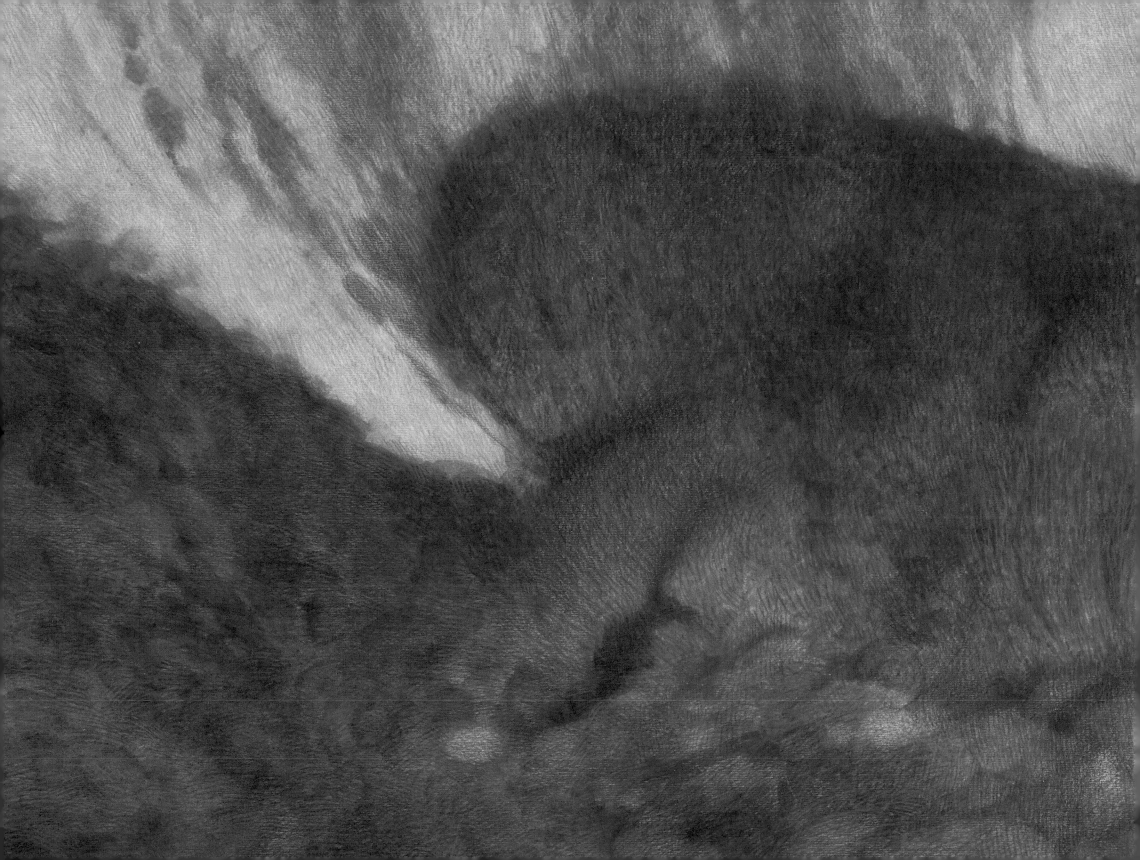

The hermit crab was off by himself,
poking around in the sand, looking for
something good to eat.

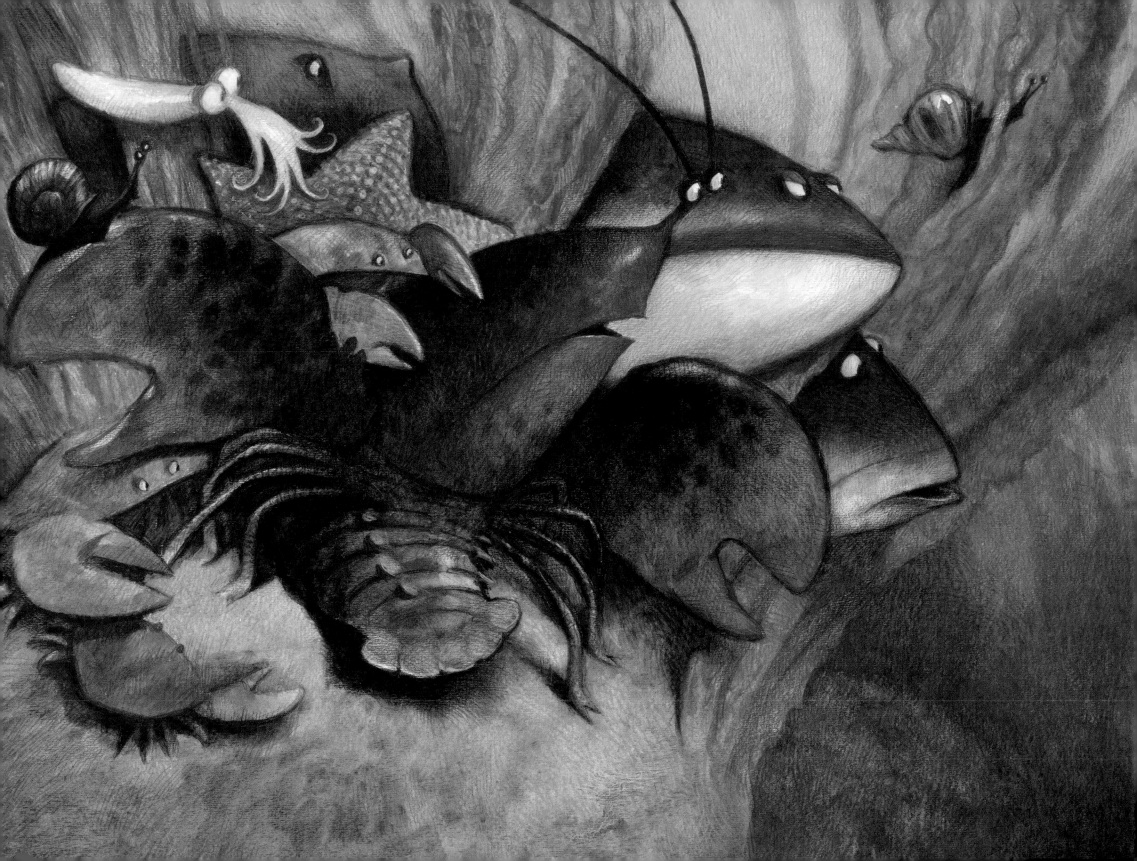

"What in the world is it?" the starfish asked.

"Some sort of new restaurant!" the lobster replied. He was sniffing at the tasty aroma that was coming from inside it.

"Stay back!" the bluefish warned. "I've seen things like this before. It smells like there's something good to eat inside, but don't be fooled; it's just a trap!"

"Hey," said the striped bass, "where's the flounder? Has anyone seen the flounder?"

Nobody had.

Meanwhile, not too far away, the hermit crab had forgotten all about looking for food. He was sitting perfectly still on top of a rock, looking down at the most beautiful shell he'd ever seen.

Very carefully the hermit crab crept over to the fancy new shell, saw that it was empty, and decided right then and there to move in.

It's even got moving parts, he thought to himself.

He felt very happy.

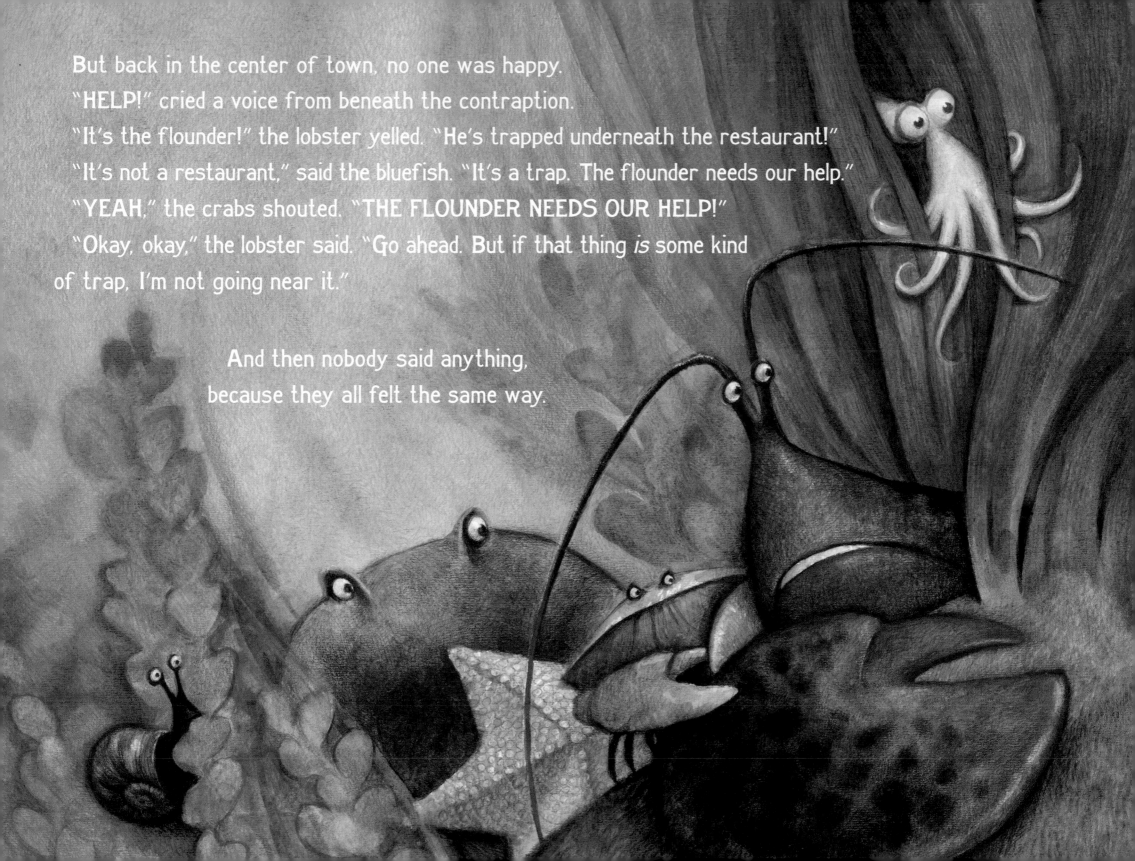

But back in the center of town, no one was happy.

"HELP!" cried a voice from beneath the contraption.

"It's the flounder!" the lobster yelled. "He's trapped underneath the restaurant!"

"It's not a restaurant," said the bluefish. "It's a trap. The flounder needs our help."

"YEAH," the crabs shouted. "THE FLOUNDER NEEDS OUR HELP!"

"Okay, okay," the lobster said. "Go ahead. But if that thing *is* some kind of trap, I'm not going near it."

And then nobody said anything,
because they all felt the same way.

The hermit crab came stumbling out of the seaweed forest, right into the center of town. *What is this?* he thought. He didn't notice the flounder, but he did notice the good smells, and that reminded him how hungry he was. He walked around the contraption, grabbing it and giving it a shake. He wanted to get in to where that good smell was coming from.

Everyone watched the mysterious stranger from their hiding places.

"Look!" whispered the starfish. "He's trying to rescue the flounder! Who IS that?"

"YEAH," the crabs shouted. "WHO IS THAT?"

"That," cried the lobster, "THAT is our brave champion! Our HERO, come to save us!"

And then, all of a sudden
the contraption moved.

Then it moved again. And finally it
began to float back into the sky.

The hermit crab was still clinging to its side. He let go at last, and gently drifted back down . . .

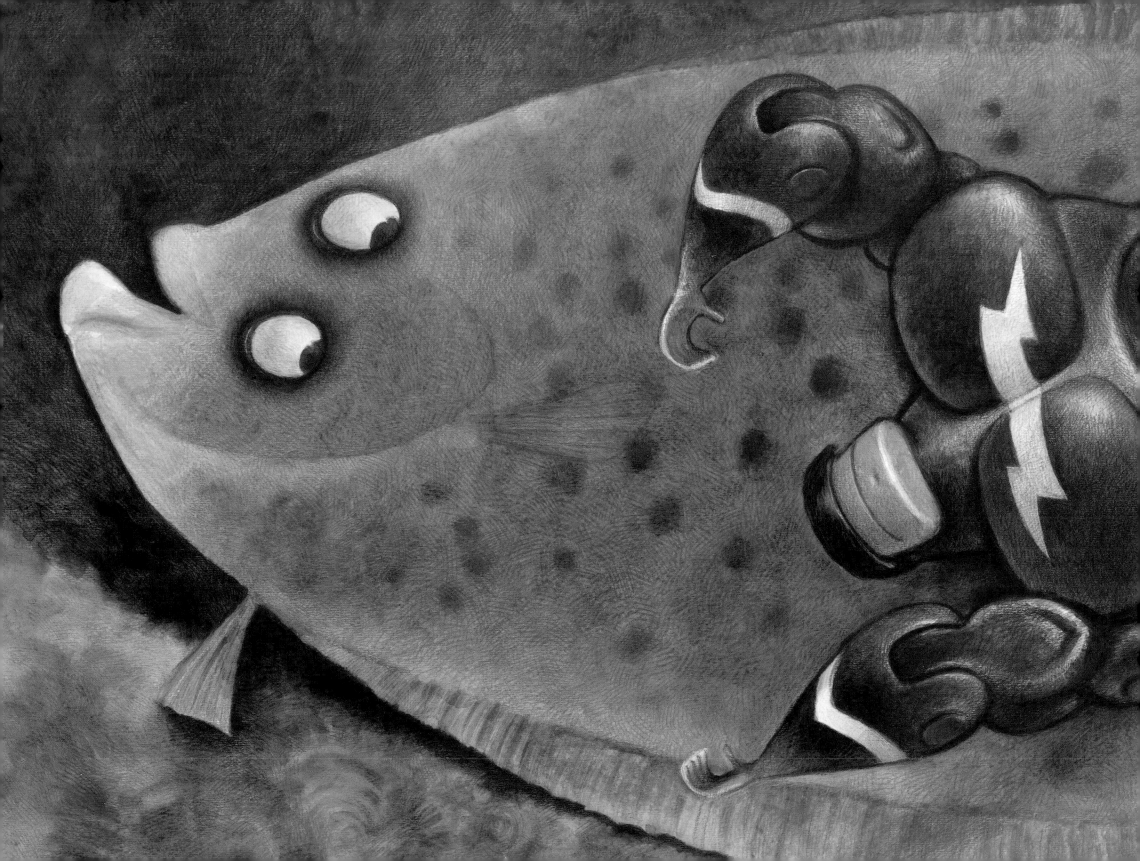

. . . and settled right on top of the flounder. The flounder, now free, tried to thank the mysterious stranger, but the hermit crab drew himself up into his new shell.

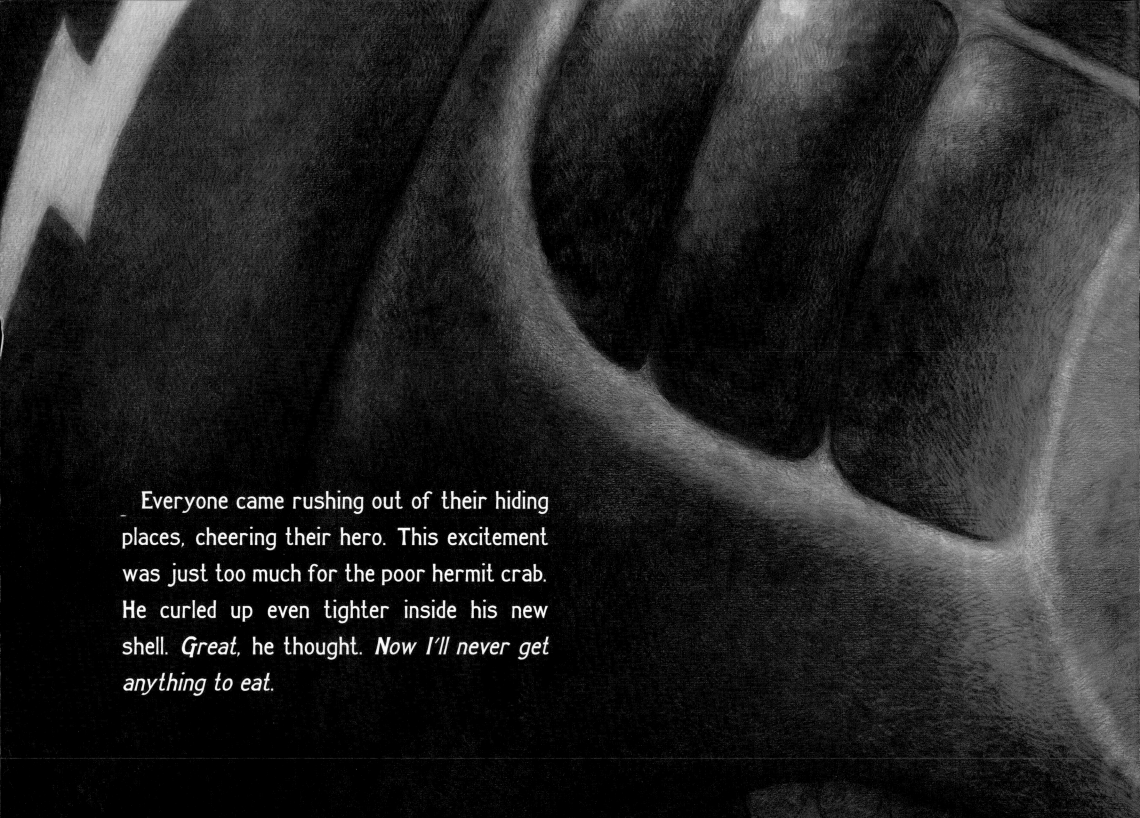

Everyone came rushing out of their hiding places, cheering their hero. This excitement was just too much for the poor hermit crab. He curled up even tighter inside his new shell. *Great*, he thought. *Now I'll never get anything to eat.*

The hermit crab's neighbors quickly organized a parade and carried their hero to the highest rock, where they carefully set him down for all to see. Then they celebrated late into the night.

The hermit crab remained hidden from view.

He tiptoed past his snoring neighbors,

As soon as it grew quiet, the hermit crab slid out of the fancy new shell.

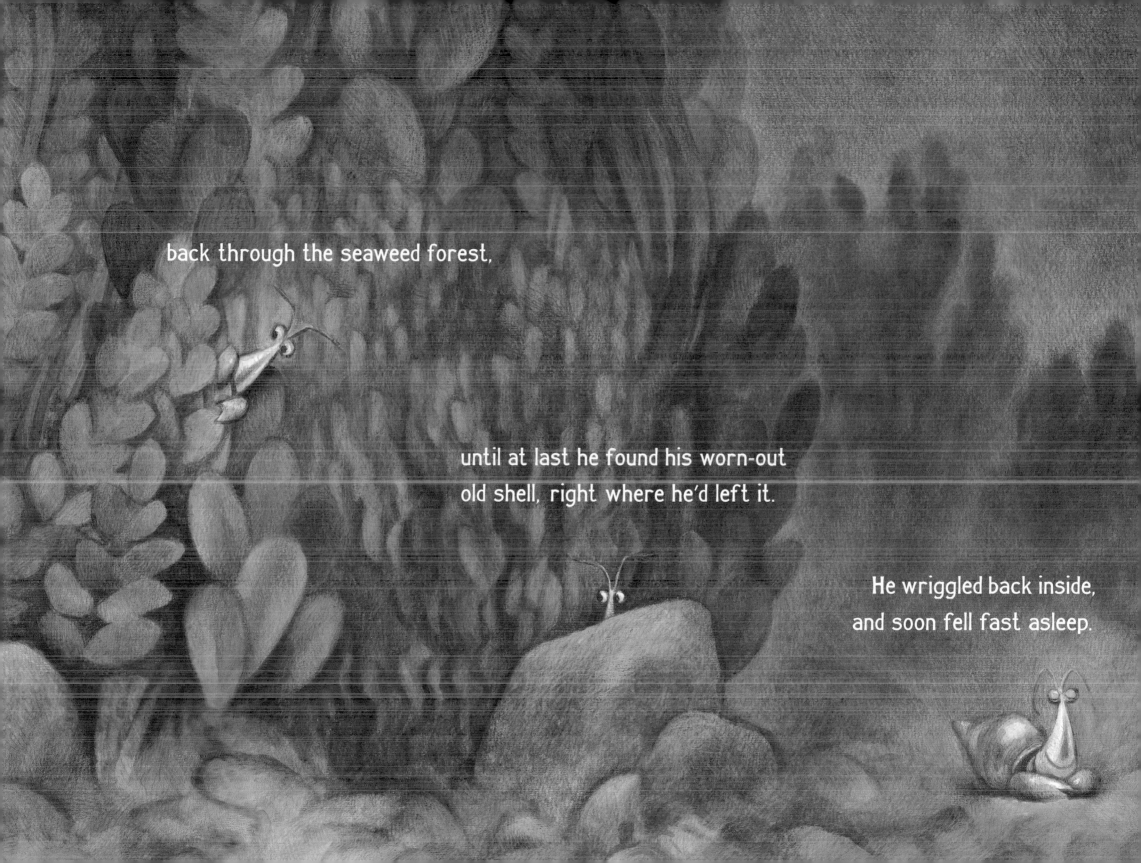

back through the seaweed forest,

until at last he found his worn-out
old shell, right where he'd left it.

He wriggled back inside,
and soon fell fast asleep.

The next day, the hermit crab made his way back to town. There, still perched on top of the highest rock, was the fancy new shell, empty as the day he'd found it. But nobody in the crowd noticed. They were happy to cheer their new hero, while the lobster made speech after speech.

So the hermit crab settled in, just beyond the edge of the crowd, right where he was most comfortable.

He smiled to himself, and he even cheered the fancy new shell. But he cheered very softly.

And just a little bit.

He didn't want to be noticed.